Dozer, the little toy bulldozer, was pushing sand around in the sandbox where he lived when KER-CLANK! Dozer hit something hard.

Created and illustrated by Karl Gude
Story by Lisa M. Combs

For Tucker, Charly, Jessica, Luke, Cullen, and Emily —
all lovers of things that GO
— L.M.C.

For Dorsey, Cole, and Erik
— K.G.

Text copyright © 1999 by Lisa M. Combs.
Illustrations copyright © 1999 by Karl Gude.

Published by WhistleStop, an imprint and registered trademark
of Troll Communications L.L.C.

Produced by Boingo Books, Inc.

Printed in the United States of America.   ISBN 0-8167-6358-5

10 9 8 7 6 5 4 3

"Check it out! Treasure!" he said
to his best friend, Jane the Crane.

Dozer backed up and went forward, and backed
up and went forward again, pushing the treasure
with all his might.

"Don't pop a gasket!" said Jane as Dozer
chugged and puffed to push the strange thing up
out of the sand.

All the machines in the sandbox zoomed over to
see Dozer's treasure. Soon they were tugging it back
and forth, arguing about what it was and who should
get to use it.

"WAIT JUST A MINUTE, HERE!" Dozer piped up.
The machines got quiet and all looked at little Dozer.
"What do you think, Bull?" Dozer asked. Bull was
Dozer's big brother, and Dozer trusted Bull to know
what to do.

Bull was proud of his little brother for finding something so exciting. But as he got closer to look at it, a scary shadow fell over the sandbox.

Suddenly, Dozer yelled, "BEAST! Beast from next door! Look out, Bull!"

Bull felt hot, smelly breath on his
roof and looked up just in time to see
dagger-sharp teeth and a slimy, wet
tongue heading straight down for
Dozer's treasure!

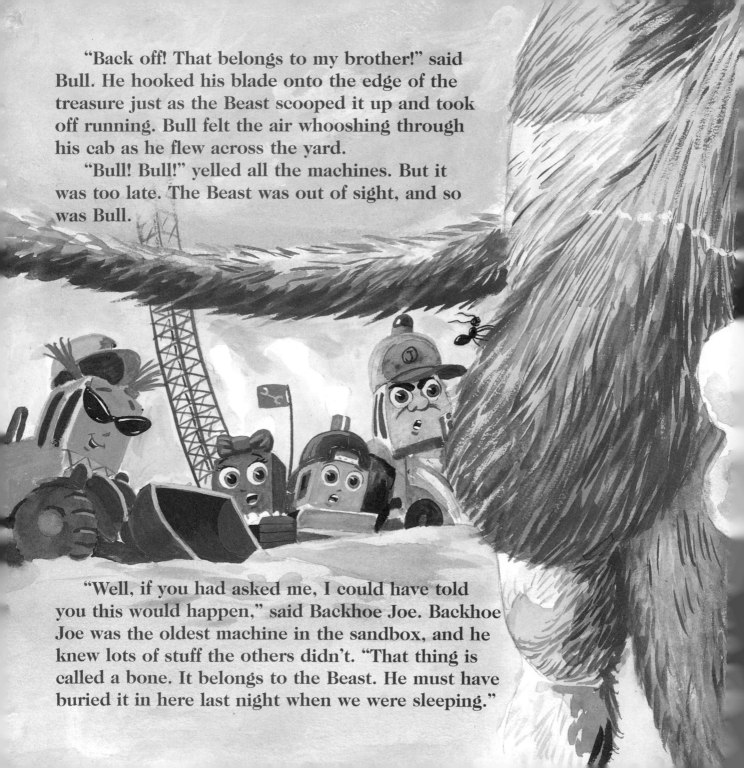

"Back off! That belongs to my brother!" said Bull. He hooked his blade onto the edge of the treasure just as the Beast scooped it up and took off running. Bull felt the air whooshing through his cab as he flew across the yard.

"Bull! Bull!" yelled all the machines. But it was too late. The Beast was out of sight, and so was Bull.

"Well, if you had asked me, I could have told you this would happen," said Backhoe Joe. Backhoe Joe was the oldest machine in the sandbox, and he knew lots of stuff the others didn't. "That thing is called a bone. It belongs to the Beast. He must have buried it in here last night when we were sleeping."

All the machines looked at the yucky puddle of Beast-slime where the treasure had been. They were sorry they had been fighting over the bone. Now they had lost Bull.

"I wish I had never found that dumb thing!" wailed Dozer.

Jane bumped Dozer kindly. "Don't worry, Dozer," she said. "We'll get him back."

"What if we found another bone?" Dozer asked. "Maybe the
Beast would come for it again and bring Bull back!"

All the earth-movers went into action! Around and around the
sandbox they dug, pushed, graded, and scooped. But no one could
find another bone.

"Give it up, guys!" cried Betsy the Bucket Loader, who got bored easily. "Let's bust out of here and go find him!" Betsy cranked up her diesel engine and tried to dig her way out of the sandbox. "Yoweeeee!" she yelled, covering her friends as she dumped.

"Oh, Betsy, you know that won't work," said Backhoe Joe, spitting sand out of his muffler. "None of us is big enough or strong enough to rescue Bull."

The machines felt sad. They knew Joe was right.

But little Dozer was thinking hard. "Wait a minute!" he said. "What if we all worked together?" Dozer pumped his pistons in excitement as he told his friends his plan.

VROOM! VROOM! VROOM! All the friends revved up their engines together! Joe scooped! Dozer pushed! Everyone else shoveled and dumped!

Finally, almost all the sand in the sandbox was piled up into a giant mountain.

"Good luck, Jane! You can do it!" the machines said as Jane the Crane chugged up the mountain. When she got to the very top, she signaled to Betsy the Bucket Loader. Betsy was the loudest of the friends, and she had a terrific whistle.

When Betsy saw Jane wave, she knew it was time to pucker up and let blow! The others all felt their metal rattle as the whistle blasted across the sandbox.

"Okay, Betsy, that's enough," grumbled Backhoe Joe. "You're about to crack my rearview mirror."

But Betsy was having a great time. It wasn't often that her friends asked her to be loud!

Betsy blew and blew until the Beast heard the awful sound. He raced over to the sandbox with the bone and Bull still in his mouth.

When the Beast got close enough, Jane the Crane went into action. With all her might, she swung her cable out to Bull. He grabbed on with his tread, and Jane let out more and more cable as Bull swung down into the sandbox and landed with a THUNK!

"Hurray!" cheered all the machines.
"Do it again!" yelled Betsy.

Dozer and Bull hooked blades in a brotherly hug.
"I'm sorry I couldn't get your treasure back, Dozer," said Bull.

"Finding that dumb bone just caused trouble with all my friends," said Dozer. "Getting my brother back is the best treasure of all! You were very brave, Bull, but I nearly threw a rod worrying about you. Please don't do anything that dangerous again."

"That's right," said Betsy. "Next time, it's my turn!"